Magical Creatures

Written by
Stephen Rickard

The world is full of different kinds of fantastic animals.

You don't have to read a story book to see magical creatures!

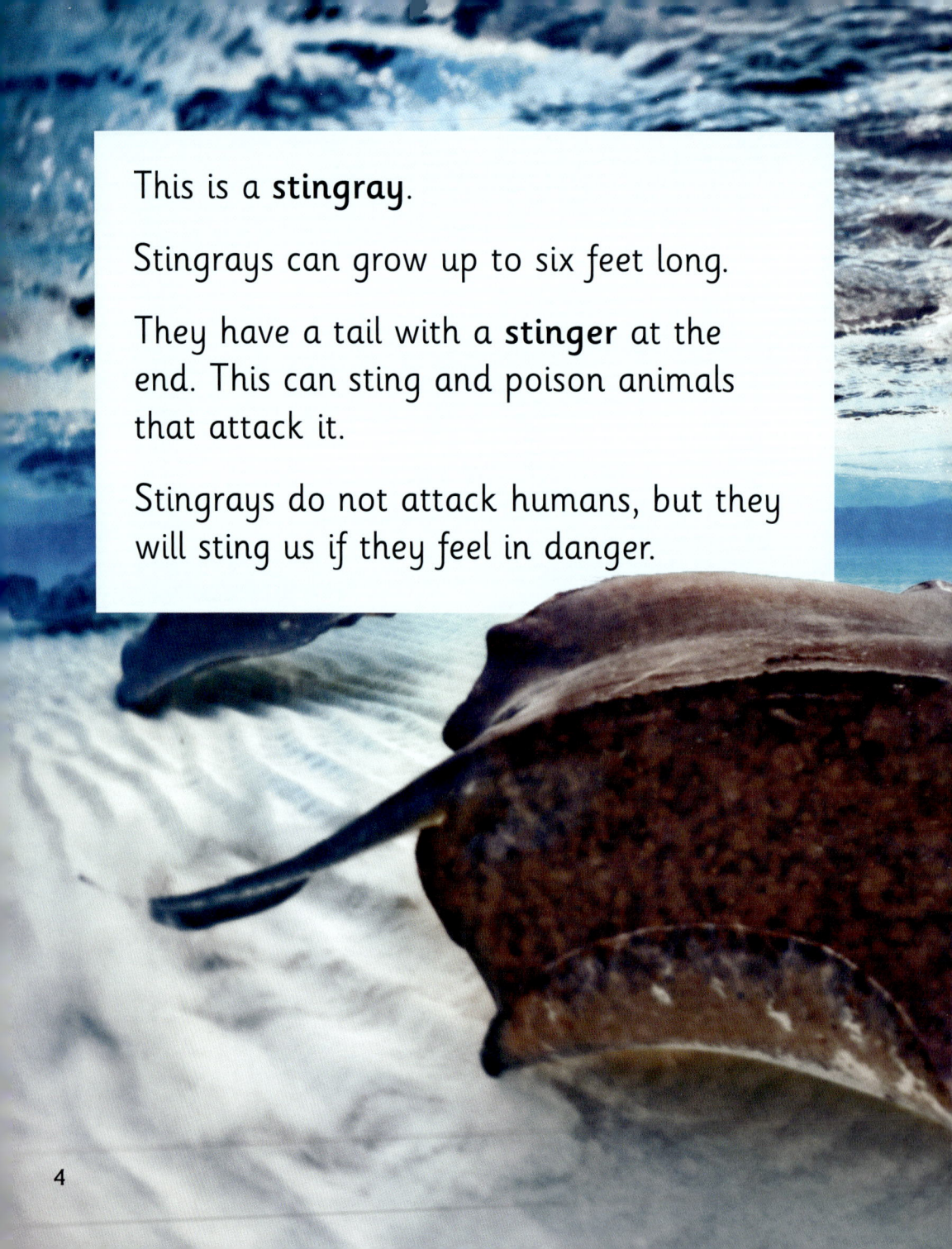

This is a **stingray**.

Stingrays can grow up to six feet long.

They have a tail with a **stinger** at the end. This can sting and poison animals that attack it.

Stingrays do not attack humans, but they will sting us if they feel in danger.

A happy stingray

Most plants make food from sunlight.
The plant makes the food in its leaves.

But the plant you can see on this page is fussy.
It likes insects. It catches insects for food.

The insects get stuck on sticky drops on the plant. Then the plant curls up around the insect and traps it.

The name of this plant is **sundew**.

This is a **thorny dragon**.
You will find it in hot places.

The thorny dragon looks odd, but it will not hurt you. It has hard, sharp spikes on its body. The spikes make it hard for an animal to grab it in its mouth.

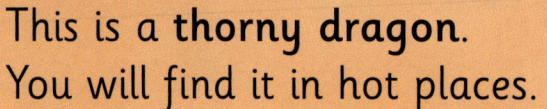

Thorny dragons are not very big.

Leafy sea dragons live in the sea.

They look like bits of seaweed drifting along.

This makes it hard for fish to see them and catch them.

This is a **squid**.

Squid are sea creatures. They have 8 arms and are strong swimmers.

They have a sharp, horny beak to kill and tear other creatures.

The biggest squid can grow up to 40 feet long.

This little lizard is called a **gecko** ("geck-oh").

Geckos have clever feet. They can run up all kinds of steep slopes. They can cling onto glass too!

The gecko's feet can stick to all kinds of things — but the feet are not sticky!

The feet have pads on them that are a bit like suckers.

The pads on a gecko's feet

There must be many magical creatures on our planet that we have not yet discovered.

This is a kind of sea slug. It was not discovered until 2002, and we don't know very much about it.